Billy's Fishing Adventure

Written By Massie Soufie

Edited By Christina Arezu Akhavan

To order additional copies of this book, contact:
Xlibris
1-888-795-4274
www.Xlibris.com
Orders@Xlibris.com

Edited by Christina Arezu Akhavan.

ISBN: Softcover   978-1-4535-6876-7

Print information available on the last page

Rev. date: 01/23/2020

This Book is dedicated to all children with special needs.
You can do anything that you put your mind and heart into.
An adventure awaits you.

The bright sun was shining through the window in Billy's room. Billy rolled over in his bed and opened his eyes. The sun was too bright and he closed his eyes again. As he was lying in bed, Billy thought to himself, what a beautiful day, if only I could go fishing.

Billy heard Mama's footsteps coming towards his room. Mama opened the door "Wake up sleepy boy. Grandpa is coming to visit!" Billy squirmed with joy in his bed, his eyes were shining. Billy loved Grandpa. Billy and Grandpa always had special times together; grandpa planned special things to do with Billy. Mama helped Billy get dressed. Billy had special braces on his legs; he could not walk without the braces.

Billy had Spina Bifida (spin-a biff-edda) it is also called open spine; Spina Bifida is a birth defect in the backbone. Every baby's spine is open when it first forms in the mother's womb. Normally it closes during the 1st month while the baby is in the mother's womb. This happens by itself. When a baby's back has not fully closed yet it is called Spina Bifida.

By the time Billy finished washing up the doorbell rang. "Hello buddy boy how are you" Said Grandpa while hugging Billy tight. Mama got Billy's fishing equipment ready. They were going fishing. Billy told grandpa,

"You read my mind, Grandpa! I was just wishing about going fishing with you!"

"Well your wish came true, let me help you get in the truck so we can start our adventure!" Billy got in the truck with Grandpa's help.

On the way to the lake they sang songs and had lots of fun. When they arrived at the lake Grandpa helped Billy to step out of the truck. Grandpa pulled the boat near the dock and helped Billy sit in the boat. Grandpa then grabbed the fishing rods, bates, and their lunch to take in the boat. Everything was finally ready. They took off for the big adventure on the lake!

Billy and Grandpa were sitting quietly with their fishing rods in their hands, when suddenly Billy heard splashing in the water. Billy looked into the water and noticed a tiny helpless turtle struggling . Billy looked at Grandpa. Grandpa moved towards Billy's side and they both looked in the water. Billy's eyes were shining.

"Grandpa, I think the turtle is hurt," Billy said.

"He sure is buddy boy, it seems that his foot is bleeding." exclaimed Grandpa.

"Can we help him Grandpa? Can we?" cried Billy.

"We need to pull him out of the water first to see what has happened to him," said Grandpa.

Billy was thinking about how they could help the turtle. He remembered that Grandpa had an old fishing net in his boat. So he told Grandpa about his plan. "That is a wonderful idea buddy boy!" said Grandpa happily.

Grandpa took the old net out and threw it in the water. Billy helped Grandpa and together they pulled the turtle up into the boat. The turtle was afraid because he had his head in his shell. Sadly, his bleeding foot was hanging out of his shell.

Billy felt very sorry for the turtle. He wanted to help him. He asked Grandpa if they could use the first aid kit to put some medicine on the turtle's foot. Grandpa thought it was a great idea, but the turtle's injury was serious, and the medicine from the first aid kit would not be enough. Billy and Grandpa looked at each other. They had the same idea. The turtle needed a veterinarian.

They decided to postpone their fishing trip and take care of the turtle first. Grandpa took the boat back to dock. They took their fishing equipment back to the truck and Billy kept the turtle on his lap wrapped up in a towel. Grandpa put some ointment on the turtle's foot to keep him comfortable until they reach the nearest veterinarian's office.

When they reached to the veterinarian's office, Grandpa helped Billy gently move out of the truck while Billy held the turtle tightly.

Billy saw a variety of animals at the veterinarian's office: Dogs, cats, birds, even a snake was there for treatment.

Billy and Grandpa sat and waited patiently for their turn. When they were finally called in, Billy was thankful to see the veterinarian because he knew that the veterinarian would help the turtle. The veterinarian checked the turtle and had a talk with Grandpa and Billy. The veterinarian said that the turtle needed to have an operation and needed to stay until he was ready to go back in the water.

Billy picked a name for the turtle. Billy chose the name "Lucky", because the veterinarian told Grandpa that the turtle was very lucky for being found right in time to save his foot. Billy and Grandpa left the turtle at the veterinarian's office, and headed home.

On the way home, Billy could not stop thinking about Lucky. As soon as he reached home, Billy told Mama about his adventure. Mama was so excited that Billy helped an animal.

Mama told Billy about the day he was born. The doctors told her that Billy had Spina Bifida and they would have to operate on him. Everybody in the family was concerned and hoping that Billy's operation would go fine. Billy felt the same for the turtle as his Mama and family did for him. Billy knew that he had Spina Bifida and could not walk, but he was happy and thankful that he is able to be with Mama and Grandpa.

Finally, the big day had arrived. Billy and Grandpa were ready to go pick up Lucky. When they reached the veterinarian's office they went inside hoping for good news. The veterinarian did have good news for Grandpa and Billy. The operation was a success and Lucky could go back into the water. Billy and Grandpa took Lucky back into the truck and headed for the lake. While grandpa was driving back to the lake, Billy began talking to Lucky. Lucky was not afraid of Billy, his head was out of his shell and he was listening and looking at Billy with a big smile.

When Billy and Grandpa reached the lake Grandpa helped Billy back into the boat while he carried Lucky in his hands. Lucky stayed in Billy's hands until they reached the same spot that they found him. There Billy kissed Lucky, returned him back into the water and said goodbye. Lucky had a mom and dad and a family of many little turtles waiting for him. Lucky would be happy to see his family. The lake was Lucky's home, where Lucky belonged. Lucky was free in the water and Billy was happy that his friend was able to swim again.

After Billy said goodbye to his friend Lucky, Billy and Grandpa decided to continue the rest of their fishing adventure. With Grandpa's help, Billy set up his fishing gear, sat with Grandpa in the boat and waited. They talked about how happy they were for Lucky and his family to be together again. Looking over the peaceful water Billy could not believe how exciting it was to help Lucky get better.

When he least expected it, Billy felt a tug at the end of his fishing pole! "I've got one!" he exclaimed. "Reel it in, Billy Boy!" Grandpa said with a big smile. They worked together to pull the line in and were shocked to see the size of the big fish that Billy had caught! The big fish wiggled, squirmed, and flopped all over the place! They marveled at the size of the fish. Grandpa snapped a photo of Billy and the big fish, and then they set the fish free back into the water.

After all the excitement, Billy and Grandpa packed up to head home. The whole drive home Billy could not stop thinking about his adventures with Lucky and catching the big fish. He was so happy and knew that Mama would be so proud of him, and she was.

As soon as they got home, Billy and Grandpa showed Mama the picture and described to her just how big the fish was. Mama was so proud and decided to put the picture on the mantle right above the fireplace that way everyone could always see it. Billy knew he would never forget this fishing trip – fun times with Grandpa, meeting Lucky and saving his life, and catching the biggest fish in the water! What an awesome day.

An adventure awaits you.

Tips for Teachers

This book and the questions below can serve as a complete lesson plan, so the children would have a better understanding of not only Spina Bifida, but also some of the words and terms related to Spina Bifida.

1. Explain the nature of Spina Bifida.
2. Explain birth defects and talk about some common births defects in children.
3. Talk to the children about the words "disabled", "disability" and "mobility".
4. Discuss different types of disabilities in children.
5. Describe the Spinal Cord and its functions in the human body.
6. Illustrate Leg braces, walkers, wheelchairs or any other related items children with Spina Bifida might use.
7. Describe what an occupational therapist does for children like Billy.
8. Describe veterinarians and what they do.
9. Ask the children to talk about any adventure that they might have.
10. Ask the children to draw and write a story of their own adventure.
11. Ask the children why Billy released the turtle back into the water.
12. Ask the children why Lucky was alone when Billy found him.
13. Why did Billy release the fish that he caught back into the water?
14. Ask the children to draw pictures of their favorite parts of Billy's Fishing Adventure.
15. During circle time, ask the children to tell the story of Billy's Fishing Adventure from their own pictures.

Printed in the United States
by Baker & Taylor Publisher Services